My Dad's a Policeman

Cathy Glass has been a foster carer for more than twenty-five years and has three children. She uses the name Cathy Glass for writing purposes only and this is her ninth book. To find out more about Cathy and her story, visit www.cathyglass.co.uk.

Also by Cathy Glass

True Stories

Cut
The Saddest Girl in the World
I Miss Mummy
Damaged
Hidden

Fiction

The Girl in the Mirror

My Dad's
a Policeman

Cathy Glass

This novel is entirely a work of fiction. The names, characters and incidents portrayed in it are the work of the author's imagination. Any resemblance to actual persons, living or dead, events or localities is entirely coincidental.

HarperElement
An Imprint of HarperCollins*Publishers*
77–85 Fulham Palace Road,
Hammersmith, London W6 8JB

www.harpercollins.co.uk

and *HarperElement* are trademarks
of HarperCollins*Publishers* Ltd

First published by HarperElement 2011

1 3 5 7 9 10 8 6 4 2

A catalogue record of this book is
available from the British Library

ISBN 978-0-00-737475-5

Printed and bound in Great Britain by
Clays Ltd, St Ives plc

Mixed Sources
Product group from well-managed
forests and other controlled sources
www.fsc.org Cert no. SW-COC-001806
© 1996 Forest Stewardship Council

FSC is a non-profit international organisation established to promote the
responsible management of the world's forests. Products carrying the FSC
label are independently certified to assure consumers that they come
from forests that are managed to meet the social, economic and
ecological needs of present or future generations.

Find out more about HarperCollins and the environment at
www.harpercollins.co.uk/green

My Dad's a Policeman

Chapter One

My dad's a policeman and it can land me in trouble. Take last week, for example. A kid on our estate shouted: 'Your dad ain't a policeman! You're a bastard, same as rest of us.' So I hit him, not hard, but enough to send him crying to his mother, who called the police.

'Oh, Ryan,' my mum sighed, exhausted, when she opened the front door two hours later to find the police there. 'Whatever have you done now?'

At that moment I really regretted hitting that kid. Not because he hadn't deserved it – no one says things about my dad and gets away with it. But because of the look on Mum's face. She was so sad I thought she was going to burst into tears, and I knew it was my fault. She didn't need more trouble from me, not with everything she had to cope with.

'I'm sorry, Mum,' I said as she let the two officers into the hall. 'Some kid got to me with something he said about my dad.'

'But Ryan you've never known your father! Why do you pretend you do and make up things about him?'

I shrugged, looked at the ground and felt pretty small.

'Say sorry to the police,' she said. 'Then tomorrow you can apologise to the boy.'

'I'm sorry,' I said to the two officers, 'I promise it won't happen again.' But I knew from the glance they exchanged my apology wasn't going to be enough this time. I'd said sorry to them when I'd been in trouble before and then got into more trouble.

I also knew that if the police told social services that I'd been in trouble again it would be my fault if my brother and I ended up in care.

'It's not your fault,' the social worker said. This was a week later, and she was smiling at me over her Ted Baker half-rimmed glasses. 'Even without that incident with the boy, or the fire last night, the situation could not have carried on.

'All the agencies involved in your case feel it's in your and your brother's best interests to come into care for a while. It will give your mother a chance to sort herself out. She's had quite a lot to cope with and this decision will help her.'

I stared at the social worker. She's called Sarah Duffy, but Mum and me have nicknamed her Duffy for short. I didn't say anything. I knew if I said what was in my head it would make things even worse.

Her comment about my mum sorting herself out had really bugged me, plus I was cross at the suggestion Mum would do better without my brother and me living with her. You can't talk to social workers; they listen but they don't hear. My mum had tried talking to social services and look where it got her!

'I do understand how you must be feeling, Ryan,' Duffy continued. She spoke in the same patronising, dead-beat tone. 'But aged twelve you are a minor and need to be looked after.'

She gave a funny little sniff, which made her glasses twitch, then waited for me to agree. I hoped she found my silence unsettling or even menacing. Social workers love to talk and Duffy could talk for England. I know, I've listened to her rabbiting on to Mum.

'So there's nothing for you to worry about,' she said after a while. 'I'll take you to your foster home shortly. Then I'll call round and see your mum and get some of your things. If I've got time this evening I'll bring your things to you. If not, I'll bring them first thing in the morning.' Duffy smiled and sniffed again. Then she looked at the folder she had open on the table.

I wondered how old Sarah Duffy was and if she was married with kids of her own. I tried to picture her kissing her old man or even having sex, but my imagination didn't stretch that far.

'Your foster carer is called Libby,' she said, reading from a print-out. 'I don't know her myself but I'm sure she's a very nice lady. It says here that she has looked after lots of boys your age. You'll have your own room and plenty to eat. If you have any worries you can ask her or phone me. I'll give you the number to call before we leave.' She looked at me and waited again.

I had the urge to smack her silly face – not just for what she was doing to me but for what she was doing to my mum. I knew my mum would be gutted when they told her my brother and me had been taken from school into care. My mum often says my brother and me are the only reason she carries on living, and now Duffy was taking us away.

'Where's Tommy?' I asked at last, speaking for the first time since I'd come into her office.

'Your brother is with another social worker,' Duffy said. She was smiling, clearly feeling she was getting somewhere and that my talking was real progress. 'He's going to a foster home not far away from yours. Once you're both settled with your foster carers, I'll arrange for the two of you to see each other – later in the week.'

'Later in the week!' I said, shocked. 'Tommy's my brother. We have to stay together. I look after him.'

'I know, pet,' she said, dead patronising, 'but my manager and I feel the needs of you and your brother would be best met if you had different placements. Tommy is young enough to make a fresh start.' Read: you're a bad influence on him.

'Fresh start!' I said, my voice rising. 'What are you talking about? Tommy's my little brother. He doesn't need a fresh start!' I was starting to feel all hot and bothered, like I did when that kid said my dad wasn't a policeman, or when the maths teacher told me to shut up and sit down and I hit him. I felt the heat creep up my spine and it made me twitchy. I knew I had to calm down; otherwise I was going to do something I would regret. And that would make things a lot, lot worse.

'I can't go without my brother,' I said, taking a deep breath, and trying to be as calm as I could be. I heard my voice shake slightly – from anger or fear? 'I promised my mum I'd look after Tommy,' I added. 'I can't let her down again.'

'You're not letting your mum down, Ryan,' Duffy said, fixing me with her patronising, half-rimmed Ted Baker gaze. 'Try not to worry. It's for the best. Your brother will be well looked after, I promise you.'

'What, like you promised my mum that if she worked with you and tried to stop drinking you'd keep our family together?' I could feel the heat rising and settling in the back of my head. My feet began to drum beneath the table.

'I did my best, Ryan,' Duffy said, a little too easily, like maybe she hadn't. 'But, as you know, your mum didn't keep to the rehab programme. We gave her a year to stop drinking but nothing changed, did it? If you hadn't woken last night and smelt smoke coming from your mum's bedroom you could have all died. I understand your mum fell asleep with a cigarette—'

'I'm not going anywhere without my brother,' I said tightly, interrupting. I could feel my teeth clench as panic rose. 'If you have to take us away from my mum, then please keep us together.'

Duffy was quiet for a moment and when she spoke she was slightly subdued. 'I'm sorry, Ryan, the decision has been made.'

'My brother needs me,' I blurted. 'He's only five. You must place us together, please, or I'll tell my dad.'

I saw the faintest hint of a smile flicker across her face at my last comment, about my dad. I tried to calm the rage flaring inside me and had she not said anything more I might have managed it. I might have been OK and calmed down.

But the silly moo thought either I was dim and didn't understand what she was saying, or that I needed a reality check. Duffy continued: 'Ryan, pet, you're not in contact with your father, and as far as I'm aware you never have been. Although I can of course appreciate why a boy of your age would like to believe he is. '

For a moment I felt strangely calm, as though someone had just pulled out my fuse. When I spoke, my voice had lost its tremble and sounded calm too, almost too calm – controlled. 'My dad's a policeman,' I said, meeting her gaze, 'and when he finds out you've taken my brother and me into care he's going to get you, big time!'

She was smiling again, and shaking her head sadly. Then she added something that was her biggest mistake: 'Ryan, your dad isn't a policeman. You just like to think he is and—'

That was it. She didn't get any further. The heat exploded in my brain, and a loud ringing noise filled my head. I'm not actually sure what happened next. I was suddenly on my feet, leaning over the table, and my hand landed smartly on her cheek. I heard the slap as it hit her cool, soft skin. I saw her Ted Baker glasses fly across the room, heard her scream, then the door burst open and security came in.

Chapter Two

Not long ago if you hit a social worker you got put in lock-up, but times have changed and are more laid back now. So an hour later, instead of being taken to a secure unit for juveniles, I was taken to Duffy's car, on the way to the foster carer, Libby. Poor Libby! Poor Duffy!

I could tell Duffy was uneasy about being alone in the car with me, and who could blame her? I'd hit her once and she didn't know if I would do it again. As she drove she kept glancing at me in the rear-view mirror and asking if I was OK. I told her I was, and even gave her a little smile.

Now I was calm I was genuinely sorry I'd hit her. I'm always sorry after I've lost my temper. I also knew if Mum found out I'd hit Duffy I'd be in for it big time. From what I'd overheard at social services they'd tried to find another social worker to take me to Libby's, but they were short-staffed. So because Duffy was our 'case worker', the job fell to her. I guess she drew the short straw, as Mum would say.

'OK?' Duffy asked again, glancing in the rear-view mirror, as we stopped at traffic lights.

I nodded. 'Yeah.'

'Libby only lives four miles away,' Duffy said, 'but in this rush-hour traffic it'll take us a good half hour. Are you hungry? I could stop at a McDonald's and get you something to eat.'

Duffy was trying so hard to be nice that I began to cringe. It was embarrassing. 'No, I'm all right,' I said. 'Thanks anyway.'

'Sure?'

'Yeah.'

While Duffy focussed on the road ahead, I gazed through the side window. It was nearly dark and the pavements were busy with workers going home, many of them with mobiles pressed to their ears. It was then I realised I hadn't got my phone with me. We're not allowed them in school and social had grabbed me from school that afternoon without warning.

'When you go to Mum's tonight will you get my phone, please?' I asked Duffy politely.

'I should think so,' Duffy said. 'Does your mum know where it is?'

'It's on my bed. Can you ask her to make sure it's got credit so I can phone her?'

There was short silence before Duffy said, 'We'll see,' without making eye contact in the mirror. I knew she wouldn't. Collect my phone maybe, but not tell my mum to top it up.

There's a kid in my class who's in care and he's only allowed to phone his mum on Saturdays from the foster carer's landline. When they took his mobile away, they told him phoning was part of the 'contact arrangements'. It needed to be supervised and monitored, so the poor kid only speaks to his mum once a week, with the foster carer listening.

But I was calm about Duffy's 'we'll see' and just said 'Thanks'. The reason I could be so calm was I'd already decided – even before I got in the car – that I wouldn't be staying at Libby's. As soon as Duffy left, I'd be out of Libby's and go back to Mum's. That was my plan so there was no need for me to feel upset or angry. Then I'd find out from Mum where they'd taken Tommy and rescue him.

I stared out of the window and made a mental note of the route we were following and which buses I'd need to take. It wasn't difficult. Mum can't drive so my brother and I have travelled all the buses in the area at some time. The more difficult bit would be getting on the bus without paying because I hadn't any money on me.

*　　*　　*

The clock on Duffy's dashboard showed 6.10 p.m. as we stopped outside a house in Stratford Road. It was a terraced house with a very big bush in a small front garden. All the lights were on but the curtains were closed, so you couldn't see inside.

'Libby's a lovely lady,' Duffy said again, stopping the engine. 'She's got a young boy of her own, and another foster child your age. He's been there over a year, so he's well settled. I expect you'll soon be mates. I'll see you in and sort out the paperwork. Then if there's time tonight I'll go to your mum's for your clothes.' Duffy was talking very quickly and repeating herself, and I had the feeling she was nervous. God knows why. It wasn't her who was being dumped at a stranger's without a phone and with no money.

She was still talking as we got out of the car and walked up the short front path. I heard her voice rabbiting on in the background like a trapped fly buzzing against a window trying to get out.

I was more interested in the front door. It was solid wood with no glass panels and I wondered if it was locked at night, and if so where the key was kept. With the house being terraced, the front door would be my easiest escape route. If

I went out the back I'd have to climb over fences and run across back gardens to the end of the row of houses. I didn't fancy that in the dark because there might be dogs or fishponds I could stumble into.

Duffy threw me what was supposed to be a reassuring smile and then pressed the doorbell. Immediately the door swung open, as though the owner had been watching out for us.

'Hello! Come in!' a big black woman said, welcoming us. And I mean big and black. I'm small for my age and I guess because of all the worry about Mum, and what's called lack of nutritious food, I look a bit pale – 'pasty', my English teacher said. Libby was the opposite. It was just as well we wouldn't be leaving the house together, I thought; I'd look a right prat. Not that I'm anti-black – some of my best mates are black – but if social services had tried to find a worse match for a foster mum for me they couldn't have done a better job.

'Hello! I'm Libby,' she said, grinning. 'You must be Ryan.' I thought but didn't say, Well, yes, there's only me and Duffy, so who else could I be? 'Come in and make yourself at home,' Libby said. 'So pleased to meet you, Ryan.' She was a bright, bubbly woman with wide, smiley eyes. In different circumstances I might have liked her but not now. Now I was concentrating on the exit route.

She showed us down the hall and into the front room, where the television was on with a young kid sat in front of it. 'This is my son, Brendon,' Libby said proudly. 'Brendon, this is Ryan. Say hello.'

The kid was clearly watching television and didn't want to be interrupted by the likes of me. Without turning he obeyed his mother and grunted a reluctant 'Hi'.

'Hi,' I said and hovered.

'Sit down,' Libby said, kindly.

I did as she said. The sofa was very soft and made of leather. It was a lot nicer than the one at home, which is old and stained, with a spring poking through. The room was nice, too. The wallpaper wasn't torn, and clean carpet matched the sofa and curtains. We just had lino on the floor at home. The telly was a big plasma widescreen, and there was a Sky box on the shelf beneath. Her kid looked happy, clean and well–fed. Just for a moment, for a second before I caught myself, I felt angry with Mum for not making our house like this, instead of drinking herself senseless every night.

'Callum is up in his room,' Libby said, smiling at me.

'Callum is Libby's other foster child,' Duffy explained, making herself comfortable in the matching leather armchair.

While they talked, and then filled in forms, I watched television. It was *The Simpsons* and I was OK with that. Every so often Duffy or Libby said something to me and I nodded. I guess it was stuff they had to tell me, like Duffy telling the school my new address, contact arrangements and something called a 'care plan'. It was only when they got near the end that my ears pricked up.

'Pocket money,' Duffy was saying. 'At Ryan's age his allowance is £8.50 a week.'

'Yes, I'll make sure he has it,' Libby confirmed.

I looked at them. Not that I'm greedy – but with no phone and no money, £8.50 was going to be very useful. '£8.50?' I asked, wondering if I'd misheard. 'I've never had an allowance before.'

Duffy smiled, pleased that at last I was showing some interest. 'You see, Ryan,' she said, swapping a meaningful glance with Libby, 'being in care isn't so bad after all.'

I couldn't say what I was thinking because it would have got me into trouble again. I was thinking that she could shove her money and take me back home.

*   *   *

Duffy left shortly afterwards, saying she would see me later that evening or tomorrow. Libby saw her out and then came back into the room.

'Dinner's ready,' she said.

Her kid was up and out of there.

'Tell Callum dinner's ready,' she called after him.

'Callum! Dinner's ready!' the kid bellowed from the bottom of the stairs.

'I didn't mean like that,' she said. Then she smiled kindly at me again. 'Let's eat, Ryan, and then I'll show you your room. I expect you're hungry – boys of your age usually are. I've done a chicken casserole. It's not spicy.' She smiled again.

I was hungry – in fact I was starving, and my stomach was growling. But the thought of sitting and eating with her and her family while my mum was alone at home, and poor Tommy was God knows where, was more than I could bear. I suddenly felt very hot and knew I had to be alone.

'I'm not hungry,' I lied. 'Just tired. Can I have a lie-down?'

'Of course you can, love,' she said, patting me kindly on the shoulder. 'You've had quite a stressful day. I'll show you to your room. Perhaps you'll feel like something to eat later?'

I thought, again, that in a different place and time I could actually like this woman.

I followed her out of the front room and up the stairs. A kid was coming down.

'This is Callum,' Libby said as we passed. 'Callum, this is Ryan.'

He looked at me and nodded. I nodded back. He was taller than me and chunkier. He was wearing a Nike hoodie and tracky bottoms just like the ones I'd wanted for Christmas but my mum hadn't managed to save up for.

'I'll be down in a minute,' Libby called after Callum.

At the top of the stairs I followed her across the landing and she opened the door at the end. 'Make yourself at home,' she said. 'Hopefully your social worker will come with your things later. If not I have some spare that'll fit. Come down as soon as you feel ready.' She smiled again and went out, closing the door behind her.

Me, wear someone else's clothes? I don't think so!

Chapter Three

The smell of dinner floated upstairs and it smelt good. I felt my stomach cramp. I kicked off my trainers, lay on the bed and leant back. The bed was really comfortable, like the sofa downstairs. The duvet and pillows had blue stripes and looked brand new. There was even a cushioned end to rest your head on. The room had a wardrobe, a chest of drawers, a small desk with a matching chair and only one bed.

At home Tommy and me always shared the bunk beds – me at the top and him underneath. I thought of Tommy and Mum and a lump came into my throat, like I was going to cry. I knew it was my fault we were in the mess we were. My fault Tommy and me had been taken into care. My fault we'd been split up (I was a bad influence on him). My fault I couldn't keep out of trouble, which probably made it my fault my mum couldn't get off the drink.

Where did it all go wrong? I wondered, slipping further down the bed and staring up at the ceiling. Or perhaps my life had always been wrong, right from the start? Right from that night nearly thirteen years ago when Mum had got so drunk she was 'taken advantage of', as she put it. The following morning she couldn't even remember what the bloke had looked like. That's the trouble with drink: it rubs out your memory. So nine months later God sent her a reminder – in the form of me. With no details of my dad to prove me wrong, I decided he could be a big strong policeman, just like you see on *The Bill*. Why not? He could be.

I don't know about Tommy's dad – Mum never said who he was. But I have the feeling that Mum 'getting taken advantage of' with Tommy was worse than mine. Mum came home very drunk and beaten up one night about nine months before Tommy was born. My family isn't much different from many families on the estate – no dad, and a mum who drowns her sorrows in a bottle or takes drugs. In fact, men are in such short supply on our estate that they're shared – amongst the kids for repairing bikes, and amongst the mums for 'a night in with Uncle Bill'.

I must have dozed off, for suddenly there was a knocking on the bedroom door and Libby's voice saying, 'Ryan, you OK? It's nine o'clock. Can I come in?'

'Yeah.' I struggled up the bed.

The door opened and Libby came in, carrying Mum's old suitcase. I stared at it surprised. It was kept in the cupboard under the stairs at home. The last time she'd used it was when she'd gone into hospital to have Tommy.

'Your social worker dropped your things by earlier,' Libby said, smiling. 'We decided not to wake you as you were fast asleep. Sarah said to tell you she saw your mum and she's fine and sends her love.' Libby crossed the room and put the suitcase by the bed.

Mum's fine and sends her love? What the hell was she talking about? Mum wouldn't be fine; she'd be out of her mind with worry, very likely blotto by now. And what was Mum thinking of, sending her suitcase with my clothes in? Didn't she know I would be on my way back home soon? Suddenly I felt very rejected and sorry for myself, like Mum didn't want me.

'Are you ready for some dinner now?' Libby asked. 'Brendon has done his homework and is in bed. Callum is in the shower. My hubby, Fynn, is on the late shift, so you'll meet him tomorrow.'

I shook my head. I still couldn't face the thought of eating strange food in a stranger's house, and I always did us fish fingers and chips on Wednesdays at home.

'All right, love,' Libby said kindly. 'You'll have to make up for it at breakfast. You'll feel better after a good night's sleep and with some of your things around you.'

I nodded but couldn't look at her. Sorry, Libby, I thought, I won't be here for breakfast.

'Would you like some help unpacking?' she asked kindly.

'Na, I'll see to it.'

'All right, if you're sure. If there's anything you need just let me know.

'There is one thing, Libby,' I said, hoping my voice wouldn't give my thoughts away.

'Yes, love?'

'Duffy, I mean my social worker, said about my allowance. Could I have it, please?'

'What, now?'

'Yeah, if that's OK.'

'But you won't have anything to spend it on tonight.'

I realised Libby was a bit sharper than I'd given her credit for, probably from years of looking after kids like me, but I could be sharp too. 'My social worker's sent my phone,' I said, 'and I need to top it up so I can phone my friends. I'll just pop to the corner shop. I won't be long.'

'And your social worker knows you have your mobile?'

I nodded. 'I asked her to bring it. It'll be in the case.' Whether it was in the case or not I didn't know, but I didn't think Libby would challenge me – not when I'd just arrived.

'Saturday is usually pocket-money day,' she said, 'but I can let you have it early this week. However, I'd rather we stopped off at the shop on the way to school in the morning, than you go out now. It's getting late. I'll be taking you to school in the car, so we'll just leave a bit earlier. If you want to talk to your friends now, you can use the landline in the front room – as long as you're not phoning Australia.' She gave a little laugh and I realised I was beaten. I'd have to go back to plan A – do a runner once she was in bed.

Libby disappeared and then returned ten minutes later, to my delight, with £8.50 and a glass of water. 'Here,' she said, tucking the money under my pillow, 'keep it safe until morning. You'll feel better knowing it's there.' Nice lady! I thought. 'And have a drink,' she said. 'You need a drink, even if you're not hungry. I've put a towel for you in the bathroom; the bathroom's straight across the landing. Shall I show you around the house now, or do you want to wait until tomorrow?'

'Tomorrow, please. I'm very tired.' I yawned to prove the point.

'All right, love. Goodnight.'

'Goodnight, Libby.'

As soon as the door closed I slipped off the bed, opened Mum's suitcase and began digging through it for my phone. I caught a whiff of the musty smell that's always in our house – a mixture of damp and stale booze – and it made me feel very homesick. I continued searching for my mobile.

I'd never seen all my clothes together before. They were normally strewn around the bedroom or waiting to be washed. Seeing them all together made me realise how scruffy I must look compared to Brendon and Callum, or the kids at school. Mum had packed my other school trousers but they were filthy, and so was the pair I was wearing. I dug to the bottom of the case; then tipped it upside down, but there was no phone. Shit! Whatever was Mum thinking? But at least I had the £8.50 so I had bus fare home.

Chapter Four

I sat back down on the bed and watched the clock on the wall. Ten minutes passed and I heard Callum finish in the shower and go to his bedroom. Everything went quiet.

At ten o'clock Libby came up and called: 'Goodnight, Callum,' from outside his door.

He called back: 'Night!'

It went quiet again and I wondered if Libby had gone to bed. She said her old man was on lates, so as soon as Libby was in bed asleep I could escape. I needed a pee, which would give me a chance to check things out.

Crossing my room, I opened the door. The landing light was on but the house seemed quiet. I crossed the landing to the door opposite, which Libby had said was the bathroom, and pushed open the door. The extractor fan came on with the light to reveal a gleaming, sparkling white bathroom. So clean and white it looked like something from a TV ad. There was a big mirror over the basin, and when I lifted the lid on the bog there was nothing horrible stuck to the sides.

I had a pee, flushed it and washed my hands. There was a clean blue towel neatly folded over the bath and I guessed it was the one Libby had said she'd put in here for me. I dried my hands and, as I did, I caught a glimpse of my face in the mirror. I looked even paler than I normally did – grey almost. Hardly surprising with everything that was going on, I thought. I opened the bathroom door and switched off the light.

Libby appeared from the top of the stairs in her dressing gown and slippers. 'You all right, love?' she asked, smiling warmly.

'Yeah. I needed a pee. I'm off to bed now.'

'OK. I won't be late either – I'm done for.' She smiled again and hesitated, and I had the feeling she would have liked to give me a big hug. I hoped she wouldn't get into trouble with the social when she found me gone in the morning.

I lay on the bed again, watched the clock and waited. I wondered about the other foster kids who had slept in this room – the other kids she'd fostered. Why were they in care? It was 10.45 p.m. when I heard Libby come up the stairs, the landing light click off and her bedroom door close. I gave her another fifteen minutes; then I quietly slithered off the bed and put on my trainers.

I could feel my heart thumping in my chest, and I also felt strangely light-headed, probably from not having eaten all day. I took a couple of swigs of the water Libby had left for me, then began creeping slowly and quietly across the carpeted floor. I switched off the bedroom light before I opened the door. I paused and listened, my hand on the door ready to close it if I heard anything, but all was quiet. Fortunately Libby had left a night light on, so the landing and stairs weren't completely dark.

I took one step on to the landing and paused and listened again. Still quiet; not a sound. I turned and slowly closed the bedroom door. I didn't want anyone going to the bathroom in the night and discovering me missing. The longer I had to get away the better.

With my heart thumping and my mouth dry, I crept across the landing and began moving carefully down the stairs. Thank God Libby had carpet everywhere. You couldn't have done this at my house – the lino would have given you away. There was still enough light coming from the landing to see the hall and front door. I saw the chain and the bolt on the front door, and then the lock with the key still in it.

Someone was on my side and watching over me!

Very carefully, hardly daring to breathe, I crept up to the door and unhooked the chain. Then I knelt down and leant against the door with my shoulder, so that the bolt slid out of its barrel easily and noiselessly. There was just the key now. Libby was certainly one for security! Straightening, I took the key between my thumb and forefinger and slowly turned. It was stiff, but then it suddenly went with a loud click. I glanced up the stairs behind me as I pulled open the door. The cold night air rushed in.

Then I was on the path, quietly closing the door; then running like hell down the pavement. Down Stratford Road and left at the top. I felt the cold air catch my throat. First right and I was on the High Street, which was quiet at 11 p.m. on a weekday. I slowed to a walk; if a police patrol car saw a kid my age running along the street late at night they'd stop. I know this, as most of my mates have been picked up at one time or another late at night; some of them make a habit of it.

I arrived at the bus stop. I was the only person waiting, and I'd no idea how long it would be before a bus came. There'd been a timetable in a glass case fixed to the bus stop at some point, but it was long gone. The glass was broken and the case filled with rubbish – chewing gum and fag ends. The February night air was freezing and I only had on my old school jacket, no coat. I wondered if I should walk to the next stop to keep warm, but the bus might come when I was between stops, so I decided to wait. I drew up the collar on my jacket and pulled in my head. Cars passed every so often but no bus came. I knew the 247 was supposed to run every twenty minutes, so I decided I must have just missed one.

Another couple of minutes passed. Then a flashy silver car pulled into the kerb and the driver lowered his window. He was middle aged, fat, bald and slimy. I knew immediately what he was after.

'You look cold, little boy,' he said, leering. 'Can I give you a lift?'

'Na.'

'I'd make it worth your while.'

I drew my head deeper into my jacket and turned away.

'How does twenty quid sound and a lift to wherever you want to go?'

My blood boiled. I span round and kicked his car. 'Piss off, you pervert! My dad's a policeman.'

I kicked the car again. He made a V sign as his window rose and he sped away. That's the trouble with being my age: the world is full of pervs like him.

Two minutes later and, to my relief, the 247 bus came into view. All the lights were on and it looked so warm and welcoming. I've never been so pleased to see a bus before. I was going home. It drew to a halt and the doors swished open. I stepped on to the platform and dug my hands into my trouser pockets. It was then I realised I'd left the £8.50 under the pillow at Libby's!

'Bollocks!' I cursed. Then to the driver: 'I've left me money at home.'

He tutted. 'You're a bit young to be out this late.'

'I've been visiting a sick relative,' I lied.

He tutted again. 'I've seen you before on the buses, with your brother. You live on the Pellinger Park estate, don't you?'

'Yeah. That's where I'm going. Sorry, can I pay you another time?'

He was a decent guy and I guess he felt sorry for me. He nodded. 'Hop on.'

'Thanks, mister. I'll pay you as soon as I can.'

Chapter Five

Half an hour later the bus pulled into the terminus at the end of my estate, and me and a woman with a bloke got off. I vaguely knew the woman but she was too busy necking with the bloke to notice me. I'd never been out alone on the estate this late before; only the crackheads with their dogs were out now. It was dark, even with the street lamps on, and I ran flat out, taking the short cuts down the alleys, until I got to my row of houses. It's called Conker Terrace, although there's not a tree in sight. I live at number nine. I went round the back – we always use the back door, although I knew Mum would have locked it by now.

The light was on in the living room and, as I looked through the window, I could see Mum sitting on the sofa staring at the telly, but it wasn't switched on. She was so still and starey that for a moment I thought she might be dead. But then I saw the empty bottle by her chair and realised it was the drink. I tapped on the glass and she jumped. As she turned I saw the pain and fear in her eyes in the second before she saw it was me. Then it changed to relief and a different sort of pain – like her heart had been broken in two.

'Ryan!' she cried as she opened the door, flinging her arms around me. 'Ryan, my baby!' She squeezed and hugged me for all she was worth. I smelt the booze and felt her unsteady on her feet. I wrapped my arms tightly around her and buried my head in her shoulder. I knew she wasn't perfect, but she was my mum and I loved her dearly.

We went inside and she shut and locked the door. Then we stood hugging for some time. She was the same height as me but thinner; the booze saw to that – she never ate. After a while I felt her pull away. Although she'd been drinking she wasn't drunk, her words weren't slurred and her mind was astute.

'How did you get here, son?' she asked, anxiously.

'Bus.'

'From where?'

'Other side of town. Didn't they tell you where they were taking me?'

Mum shook her head and her brow creased. 'All they told me was that you'd be safe and well cared for, and that was all I needed to know. The social workers said you'd be put with carers in the area so that you could go to the same school. There were two of them: Duffy and someone new.'

'Mum, where's Tommy?'

She shook her head again, and tears sprang to her eyes. 'They wouldn't tell me. They said he would be staying in the area but at a different address to you. I said if the social had to take you both into care, then couldn't they keep you together? They said it wasn't possible, that they didn't have a carer who could take both of you, and anyway it was better if you were apart.' She was crying openly now, and looked so tired and old – far older than she should have done. She was only thirty-three but already had lines and grey hair – a mixture of booze, fags and worry, I guess.

I suddenly felt shivery and dizzy, like I might faint.

'You all right, son?' Mum asked.

'Na.' I went to the sofa and sat down. The room span and there were funny jazzy patterns on the walls. 'Don't feel so good,' I mumbled.

'I'll get you a hot sweet drink,' she said. 'You eaten?'

'Na.'

'I'll get you something.'

I stayed on the sofa, trying to steady the room. There was still a faint smell of smoke from where the blanket had caught fire on Mum's bed the night before. A few minutes later Mum returned with a mug of hot chocolate and a packet of biscuits. 'Thanks,' I said, taking a gulp. It tasted good. Mum makes the best hot chocolate: she puts in extra milk and sugar. She sat next to me on the sofa while I sipped the hot chocolate and ate the biscuits. I began to feel a bit better.

'Does your foster carer know you're here?' Mum asked, rubbing her hand across her forehead.

'No. And I'm not going back.'

Mum didn't say anything and I was hurt. I wanted her to say, 'Of course you're not going back, son. You're staying here with me. Over my dead body will they take you away again!' But she didn't. She took a crumpled tissue from the sleeve of her jumper and blew her nose; then she stared at the floor.

'Mum,' I said, turning to look at her. 'Did you hear me? I'm not going back.'

She looked up at me, and her brow furrowed. 'You have to, son. They'll come and get you if you don't. It's for the best.'

'For the best! What are you talking about?' I heard my voice rise and I was starting to feel

33

hot like I do when I get angry. 'How can you say that? I'm your son. This is my home. And what were you doing sending my clothes and keeping my mobile?'

She began to cry louder, racking sobs that made her body shake. I felt sorry for her but, at the same time, I felt more sorry for me; I was the one being chucked out of my home, not her. 'They said if I did what they wanted,' she said between sobs, 'you and Tommy could go into care under a Section 20, so I would still have parental rights. They said if I didn't cooperate they would get a full care order from the court and I'd lose all say in your care. The social would become your legal parents. So I signed the forms and packed your clothes like they told me. Duffy said it wasn't a good idea for you to have your mobile, so I left it on the bed.'

Although Mum was obviously upset, what she said sounded all too easy to me – cooperating with social services and signing me over. I was her son, not some parcel being delivered to the door. What I wanted to hear was her fighting for me, yelling at the social that she'd never let her kids go into care, then chucking the social workers out of the house. But of course Mum couldn't do that: she takes the easy way out

– usually from the bottle. I was getting hotter and angrier.

Mum turned towards me, her cheeks stained with tears, and went to put her arms around me. I saw the empty bottle on the floor beside her, the stains on her clothes and the hopelessness in her face, and my anger grew.

'It's your fault!' I yelled. 'Your fault we're in this mess. Look at the state you're in! No wonder my dad didn't stick around . . .'

'Your dad?' she yelled back in disbelief. 'Your dad? Whatever has he done for you?'

'At least he hasn't messed up like you. You're a fucking disgrace. They gave you a chance to get off the booze, but you couldn't! You put that bloody bottle before your kids. You don't deserve us!' Before I could stop myself I'd kicked the bottle and it crashed against the wall. I turned and was about to kick the sofa when a loud knock sounded on the front door. I froze.

I stared at Mum and she stared back. She looked like a hunted animal – trapped and frightened. 'Who can that be at this time?' she whispered. The knock came again, louder and more insistent.

I stepped from the living room, into the short hall, with Mum by my side. Framed in the glass of the front door was the unmistakeable outline of the Old Bill. 'Shit, it's the police,' I hissed. 'Libby must have found I'd gone.' I turned and headed for the back door. Opening it, I stepped out, straight into the arms of another copper.

Chapter Six

'How did you know I was here?' I challenged
the copper as he herded me back inside.

'Your foster carer reported you missing. It's
not rocket science. Most kids who run away
from foster care go straight home.' He and the
other copper were in the living room now, and
I saw them look at the bottle and the state of
the room, then exchange a pointed glance. I
knew what they were thinking: little wonder
the kid's in care!

'I'm Chris,' the other copper said, trying to be
friendly, 'and that's Gary.' Gary, who'd caught
me out the back, nodded. 'I've seen you and
your brother before on the estate,' Chris
continued. Now he'd mentioned it he did look
familiar, but we get so many coppers on the
estate I wouldn't have recognised him. 'Your
brother's Tommy, isn't he?'

'Yeah. Do you know where he is?' I asked.
'They separated us and I'm gonna find him and
bring him home.'

'No, you're not,' Mum put in.

'Who says?' I snapped back. 'You watch me!'

'OK, OK,' Chris said, raising his voice to silence me. 'Let's not get into another argument.'

I glanced at Mum. She looked so small and fragile beside the two big, strong, smart coppers, and in the mess that was her house, I almost felt sorry for her again.

'Sit down, both of you,' Chris said. 'I'll phone control and find out what they want me to do now you've been found.'

Mum and I sat on the sofa. Chris pressed a button on the phone clipped to the front of his jacket and made contact with the police operator. I watched him as he told control I'd been found at my mother's and to advise the duty social worker they would wait with me until I was collected.

'I'm not going back,' I said, making a move to stand.

'Sit down,' Chris said, then into the phone: 'Tell the duty social worker the kid says he's not going back to his foster carer.'

'Will do,' the female voice on the other end said, and gave a little laugh. I didn't see anything funny.

Chris finished the call and turned down the volume on his phone; distorted voices crackled in the background. Chris and Gary glanced around the room; then stood a little way in front of us, trying to make polite conversation as they waited for the return phone call.

'You all right?' Gary asked Mum after a moment.

'I think I'll get a drink of water,' she said, heaving herself off the sofa. I guessed she was dehydrated from all the booze.

Gary went with her to the kitchen; perhaps he thought she was going to get something stronger than water, which was very possible. Mum always keeps extra supplies of booze in the kitchen for when she's worried and 'needs' a drink. She was obviously very worried now and the effects of the bottle she'd already drunk would be wearing off.

I've lived with Mum's drinking for so long – all my life – so I know the signs and stages. I know when she needs a drink, how much she's had and when she's going to be sick or pass out. I've cleared up more puke than I care to remember and made sure she's propped on her side at night so that she doesn't choke in her own vomit. I'm ashamed to say I've even bought booze for her sometimes when she's had the shakes so bad she can't get out of bed and begged me to.

'What team do you support?' Chris asked me, as Gary returned with Mum, who was trying hard not to slop the glass of water in her trembling hands.

I shrugged. 'Arsenal, I guess.'

'Good team,' Chris said.

'Na, Tottenham is the one,' Gary said. 'They'll give your lot a right thrashing next month.'

I shrugged again. I really didn't care who won or lost the match. I knew they were only trying to be friendly, and make conversation to put me at ease, and usually I'm OK talking about football, but not now. Now I couldn't have cared a stuff about football. I just wanted them out of here and Tommy home.

Shortly Chris answered his phone and the voice of the woman at police control crackled through: 'I've got the duty social worker on hold,' she said. 'He says the kid has to go back to the foster carer, and he can't collect him because he's on an emergency call. Can you take him there?'

'I'm not going,' I said, loudly.

The operator must have heard, for she laughed again. 'Shall I put the duty social worker on?' she asked.

'Yes, put him through,' Chris said.

A few more crackles and we heard the duty social worker say, 'Hello?'

'We're at Ryan's house now,' Chris said, looking at me as he spoke. 'He says he doesn't want to return to the foster carer.'

'Ask him why,' the duty social worker said.

Now, I could have told the truth and said: 'It's not my home and I want to be here with Mum and Tommy.' But I knew that wasn't good enough. Any kid in care would rather be at home, no matter how bad home is, rather than with a foster carer. I also knew how politically correct social workers are, especially when it comes to race.

Tommy is a bit darker than me – I guess one of his distant relatives was black. When Duffy visited us she often asked what Mum was doing to meet Tommy's cultural needs. I mean, I ask you! What crap! Tommy was just Tommy, my little brother and Mum's second 'taken advantage of'. He didn't care about his 'cultural needs'. We were more concerned with getting enough to eat. But now I wondered if I could turn their crap and use it to my advantage.

'I don't feel I fit in at Libby's,' I said, looking all forlorn. 'I don't match her. I feel right out of place there.'

Chris repeated this to the duty social worker. There was silence. Game to me, I thought. 'Ask him if he will go there tonight,' the duty social worker said, 'and we'll sort out a new placement tomorrow.'

I shook my head sadly. 'I'd rather not. It don't feel right. I can stay here for tonight.'

The duty social worker said something which I didn't catch but must have been no. Chris shook his head, and then said into the phone: 'Will do,' before turning down the volume again. 'He's going to call back when he's found you another carer,' Chris said to me. 'What was the matter with your other carer, then?'

'Nothing,' I shrugged, which was true – I just didn't want to be in care. I looked at Mum and hoped she was feeling bad, but she didn't look at me. She was staring straight ahead and avoiding eye contact. Chris and Gary started chatting again, this time about the weather and the snow that was forecast.

Suddenly I remembered my phone. I wouldn't be leaving without that again!

'Can I get a few things from my bedroom?' I asked.

'Sure,' Chris said, and nodded to Gary.

Gary came with me while Chris stayed in the living room with Mum. I saw the look of horror on Gary's face as we entered my bedroom. The room was as Tommy and me had left it, no worse, but now I saw it for what it was – a stinking tip. We didn't have a wardrobe or drawers, so our things were all over the floor in heaps and falling out of broken cardboard boxes which acted as storage. The room was littered with empty crisp packets, biscuit wrappers, fizzy drink bottles and the remains of takeaways – mainly pizza, and the room stank of piss. Tommy wets the bed – he can't help it – and I now realised I should have changed his sheets more often, but we didn't always have the money to go to the laundrette. I'd never really thought what a pit our bedroom was – lots of kids on the estate live like this – but now I felt embarrassed Gary had seen it. I bet his bedroom wasn't like this; I bet it was like the one at Libby's – clean and tidy.

Stepping over the piles of rubbish, I went to the bunk beds and climbed on to the only rung that wasn't broken. Reaching up to the top bunk, I found my phone and tucked it into my pocket. I glanced around. There was nothing else I wanted; Mum had packed the only clothes that were decent enough to wear and they were in the suitcase at Libby's.

'Anything else?' Gary asked kindly, touching my shoulder. I guess he felt sorry for me.

I shook my head, and we went back into the living room. I sat on the sofa while Gary stood a little way from Chris again. Mum was sipping the water and still not looking at me. A few minutes later Chris answered his phone and police control put the duty social worker through. I heard the duty social worker say he'd found me an emergency placement, and then ask the coppers to take me there.

'Where is it?' Chris asked. I couldn't hear the duty social worker's reply. Then Chris said: 'OK, we're on our way.'

'No, I'm not,' I said.

Chris turned down the volume on his phone and looked at me. I could tell he thought this was going to be difficult, and he was right. 'Say goodbye to your mum, Ryan,' Chris said, then, trying to joke and make it easier: 'You're going for a ride in a police car.'

'No, I'm not,' I said.

'Yes, you are,' Mum said, still not looking at me.

'No, I'm not,' I said, more forcefully.

Chris and Gary looked at me while Mum continued staring straight ahead, unable to meet my eyes. I was starting to feel a bit hot and twitchy now, like I do when I get angry. Don't lose it, I told myself; calm down. I tried to take a deep breath and count to ten like my English teacher had told me.

'I think we should go now,' Chris said, taking a step towards me. 'I'm sure your new foster carer is lovely.'

'Yes,' Mum said quietly. 'Go with them. It's for the best. She will look after you.'

'What?' I cried, rounding on her. 'Why should a foster carer look after me? You're my mother. You had Tommy and me. You should look after us, not some bloody foster carer!' I was feeling very hot now; I could feel the heat rising up my spine, making me all hot and twitchy. Calm down, Ryan, I told myself, for fuck's sake calm down or they'll arrest you.

I was still staring at Mum, fuming and blaming her. At that point I hated her so much I could have slapped her face like I had Duffy's. Then very slowly, with Chris and Gary watching, she turned and finally looked at me. Her face was grey, the lines around her mouth were deep, her brow was knitted in pain and her eyes filled with tears.

'Ryan,' she said quietly, resting her hand on my arm. 'Ryan, love, I know I should be able to look after you. Believe me, I know. I know I've failed you and Tommy dreadfully and I'm so, so sorry. You are my sons and that will never change. I love you and Tommy so much, but I can't look after you. Look at the state I'm in. It's not fair on you or Tommy. Please go quietly to your foster carer, and I will try to get better; then they might let me have you back. Go, love; go with them now. Don't get yourself into trouble. And try not to hate me.'

'I don't hate you, Mum,' I cried, throwing my arms around her and holding her tight. 'I love you. I want to stay and help you.' I felt her body jerk as she began to sob and my own tears fell. Chris and Gary stood somewhere behind us and were very quiet as I tried to soothe and comfort Mum. 'Please don't cry,' I said. 'I'll go quietly if that's what you want. Please don't upset yourself. I can't leave here with you crying.' I wanted to reassure her and tell her everything would be all right, that I'd make sure of it, but of course that wasn't so. I couldn't help her, Tommy or me, any longer. I had no say in what was happening to any of us.

'Come on, then, lad,' I heard Chris say behind me.

Mum pulled away. I looked into her tear-stained face one last time. 'Go on, son, be brave,' she said. 'Be that boy a father would be proud of.'

That was it. I couldn't bear her hurt any longer. I walked quickly towards the front door. Chris and Gary followed in silence behind me. As we left the house Mum let out the most dreadful cry. It was the worst sound I've ever heard. It was the agonising cry of a mother having her child taken away.

Chapter Seven

Policeman Gary closed the front door behind us. The other copper, Chris, unlocked their patrol car, which was parked in the kerb right outside our house. The interior light went on.

'You all right?' Gary asked me gently, placing his hand lightly on my shoulder.

I sniffed and wiped the back of my hand over my eyes. Of course I wasn't all right. How I could be? There was no point in telling Gary that; it wouldn't have done any good. Tommy was with strangers and Mum was alone, sobbing like she would die. I knew, despite what she'd said about trying to get off the drink, as soon as we'd gone she'd open another bottle – to drown her sorrows. She hadn't managed to get off the drink with Tommy and me there, so there was crap chance of her doing so now we'd been taken away.

It was nearly 1.00 a.m. and the February night air was freezing. I still only had on my old school jacket; I didn't own a coat. Chris was climbing into the driver's seat while Gary was holding open the rear door for me to get in. I glanced back at the house. I knew once I was in the car there'd be no chance of escape until I got to the new foster carer's, and then it might not be so easy this time. I needed to do something and quickly.

'You OK?' Gary asked again, holding the door open and waiting for me to get in.

I hesitated. 'I need a piss,' I said.

'OK. Hold up,' Gary called to Chris. 'Ryan needs a pee.' Then to me: 'Where are you going to go?'

'Here,' I said.

I moved away from the car, towards the house, and began fiddling with my flies. 'Don't look,' I told him, as though I was going to pee up the wall of my house. As soon as he turned his back, I legged it. I ran like the clappers down the short path to the end of our terrace, then left into the alleyway.

'Hey! Stop!' I heard him shout behind me, but I was already round the corner and going down the next alley.

I ran flat out, like the devil was after me, and perhaps he was. I could hear two sets of footsteps thundering after me down the back alleys of the estate and echoing in the silence of the night. 'Stop! Police!' Chris shouted, but of

49

course I didn't and there was no one around to hear him and intercept me.

Panting and with my face smarting from the cold, I turned right, then left, weaving in and out of the alleys like they were a maze. I knew these alleys well, much better than Chris and Gary – I'd spent my childhood playing in them. I also knew where the hiding places were, and that there was one a little further up. I made another right and left turn. Then, out of breath, I nipped into the covered recess at the end of Chestnut Close where the bins are kept. Going behind the bins, I squatted in the corner with my chin pressing onto my knees. I kept very still and tried to catch my breath.

I heard the Old Bills' footsteps draw closer, then their voices, close but muffled by the alleyways between us. My heart pounded. The pair of policemen came closer still, but before they came to where I was hiding their footsteps stopped, then began to fade away. I stayed where I was, straining my ears for any sound of them returning. I waited for what seemed like hours, but it was probably only fifteen minutes. Then I heard their car's siren as they left the estate.

*   *   *

I breathed a sigh of relief. I was safe for the time being, but very, very cold. I couldn't stay the night where I was – I'd freeze to death. And I obviously couldn't go home – the police had said the parents' home was the first place they looked for runaways. I decided now was a good time to call in a favour from my best mate, Wayne. Wayne owed me. I'd helped him a few times recently when his dad had arrived home drunk, threatening to beat him up. Now Wayne could help me out.

My hands shook from cold as I took my mobile from my pocket and opened it. The screen lit up. Thank God, I thought – at least it was charged – but I knew there was only enough credit left for a couple of texts. Like most kids my age I can usually text very quickly – with one hand and not looking at the keys. But now – with my fingers so cold – it took both hands and all my concentration to tap in the message to Wayne: *In big trouble. Need u 2 hide me. B there in 5.* I pressed the send button. Wayne would know what I meant. The message was the same as the one he'd sent me when he had to escape his father and come and stay at my house for the night (without my mum knowing).

With my mobile in my lap, I sat huddled in the corner behind the wheelie bins, my jacket pulled up around my ears, and waited. I knew Wayne would have his phone on. Everyone I know sleeps with their mobiles. Wayne and me often text each other in the middle of the night. I just hoped he'd hear the text arrive.

A couple of minutes passed and I was about to send the text again when my phone bleeped. I opened it and the screen lit up. It was a text from Wayne: *Sure man. C u in 5.* Wayne calls everyone 'man'. 'Thanks, man,' I said under my breath. I returned the phone to my jacket pocket, blew warm air into my hands and stood up.

Wayne's house is on the other side of the estate. By the time I got there he'd have crept downstairs and be waiting by the back door, just as I had done for him. Now the police were no longer chasing me I didn't use the alleys, but walked in the road, watching and listening for their return. The alleys are not the place to be late at night, as drug pushers, perverts and psychos hang out in the shadows. Last year a woman was murdered in one of the alleys late at night. People heard her screaming but were too scared to go and investigate. You don't have Neighbourhood Watch on our estate.

Wayne was waiting for me and he opened the back door as I approached.

'Thanks, mate,' I said as I stepped in. He was dressed for bed in his pants and T-shirt.

'You're welcome, man,' he whispered, and put his finger to his lips, signalling his dad was asleep upstairs.

His dad's a great fat brute and I certainly didn't want to meet him now. Wayne quietly closed and locked the back door; then I followed him silently up the stairs. The only light came from the street lamp outside but I knew Wayne's house well; we'd been mates for years and I hung out there when we bunked off school. We crept into his bedroom and he quietly closed the door. A small bedside lamp in the shape of a spaceship which he'd had as a kid was beside his bed. Wayne's room is heaps better than mine: his mum did it up a couple of years ago, just before she cleared off.

'What happened, then, man?' Wayne asked as we perched on the edge of his bed.

'Social took me and Tommy into care, but they sent us to different foster carers, so I legged it.' I decided not to tell him about the police being involved in case it spooked him. Wayne had been in trouble with the police before and I knew he didn't want any more bother with them.

'That's bad, man, real bad to split you up,' he said, sympathising. 'Hey, man, you hungry?'

which is what I always asked him when he came to my house.

'Sort of,' I said.

He reached under the bed and pulled out an Asda carrier bag, full of crisps, biscuits, cans of fizzy drinks and other junk food. I had a similar bag under my own bed. It was an emergency supply for when there was no other food in the house. I topped it up when Mum had some money, or if she didn't I'm afraid to say I nicked the stuff from the shop.

I chose a couple of packets of crisps and a can of drink from the bag, and Wayne did the same. We munched, slurped, burped and chatted – about social services taking me from school, my mum, his dad and where his mum could be. He hadn't even had a text from her since she'd run off with some bloke at work about two years before, leaving Wayne and his older sister with their drunken pig of a father. There was gossip on the estate that Wayne's father had caught up with her and done her in. It was possible: he was an evil shit. Wayne's sister has to keep her bedroom door locked at night so he can't get in.

It was nearly 3.00 a.m. when Wayne finally yawned and said: 'Hey, man, I'm knackered. Let's sleep.'

I nodded. I had hoped my mum might have phoned or texted, but I guess she was past doing either of those by now with all the drink. I didn't have enough credit to phone her and there was no point anyway if she was unconscious. I decide to send her a text so she'd find it when she woke: *Look after urself, I'm fine, luv Ryan xxx*. I wasn't going to tell her where I was in case the police asked her; Mum can't lie to save her life.

I took off my trainers, jacket and trousers, keeping on my pants, T-shirt and socks, and climbed into bed beside Wayne. This was how we always slept when he came to my house. There wasn't much room in his single bed but it was warm and comfortable. Feeling my best mate beside me after everything that had happened was reassuring. We lay flat on our backs, sides touching, and stared at the ceiling for a while.

'I'm butchered,' Wayne said, yawning again. He reached out and switched off the bedside light. 'Night, man. Fart and you're dead.'

I laughed. 'Night, and thanks.'

'You're welcome, man. What you gonna do in the morning?'

'Find Tommy.'

'Cool, man. Don't oversleep. I need you out of here before my old man's up or we'll both catch it.'

Chapter Eight

There was no chance of oversleeping. It seemed I'd just dropped off when I was woken by a loud noise. I reached under my end of the pillow for my phone and saw it was 6.20 a.m. I lay very still and listened. Wayne was fast asleep and breathing regularly beside me. The noise came again, louder this time. Then I realised with a jolt it was Wayne's old man on the bog. Their bathroom's next door to Wayne's bedroom but he could have been sitting right next to me for all the noise he was making, shitting and farting after a night on the booze. It was disgusting! Wayne slept on. I guess he was used to it, as well as the smell that seeped under the door. I heard the bog roll unravel at 100 miles an hour, then the bog flush and the bathroom door open. The dirty pig hadn't washed his hands! More worrying were his footsteps, going downstairs.

'Hey, wake up,' I hissed in Wayne's ear, poking him in the ribs. 'Your old man's up and it's only six thirty.'

Wayne groaned and opened one eye. 'Don't worry, man,' he mumbled. 'He'll go back to his room with his tea. You can get out then.'

We lay side by side on our backs again, me wide awake and Wayne slowly surfacing, as the noises of Wayne's old man making tea floated up from downstairs. The walls in these houses are so thin you can hear everything, and I mean everything. Wayne's old man is a big clumsy slob who lumbers rather than walks, so the noise he makes is amplified. I felt like Jack hiding from the giant in 'Jack and the Beanstalk' as I lay still and listened.

I heard Wayne's dad turn on the tap to fill the kettle, open a cupboard door and then set down a mug on the kitchen work surface. He did it with so much force it's a wonder the pottery didn't smash. It went quiet and I guessed he was pouring boiling water on to the tea bag. Then we heard him lumbering up the stairs and his bedroom slam shut.

'You've got until seven,' Wayne said. 'Then he comes to wake me.'

That was enough for me. I was out of bed so fast that my head span. I had on my trousers, shirt and jacket, and was stuffing my feet into my trainers, before Wayne had clambered out of bed.

'I'll see you out, man,' Wayne said, standing and scratching his balls unattractively. 'Good luck with finding Tommy.'

'Thanks.' It was then I realised I still didn't have any money. 'You couldn't lend me a tenner, could you?' I knew I was asking a lot; I couldn't have lent him money, but then he'd never asked.

'Sure, man,' he said easily. 'No problem.' I watched as he reached under the corner of his mattress and brought out a wad of £5 notes. There must have been over fifty quid there and I gasped in amazement.

'Where d'you get that?' I asked, feeling that perhaps it was better I didn't know.

'From the old man's trouser pocket, when he passes out. It's what keeps sis and me going. He don't give us anything.'

Impressed by Wayne's courage – nicking from his dad whilst he lay drunk – I accepted the two £5 notes. I wondered briefly why Wayne and his sister hadn't been taken into care, for it seemed as though their lives were as bad, if not worse, than Tommy's and mine. Perhaps social services didn't know about them, or perhaps they were too scared to confront Wayne's dad? Whatever, Wayne seemed to have the situation under control.

'Thanks,' I said, really grateful. 'I'll pay you back as soon as I can.'

'You already have, man. All the nights you put me up. Now for fuck's sake, be quiet when you go or we'll both get it.'

I followed him to the bedroom door and he slowly, silently, opened it. He paused and we listened to the sounds coming from his old man's room across the landing. The floorboards were creaking as he moved around, presumably getting dressed. Wayne signalled for me to go forwards. I tiptoed after him as he went down the stairs and to the back door. He silently turned the key and let me out.

'Take care, man,' he whispered, and closed the door behind me.

With money in my pocket and a plan of action I was now feeling pretty positive, better than I'd felt last night. First I'd walk to McDonald's in town and get myself a big breakfast – £1.99. It would be warm in McDonald's and I could stay as long as I liked. Then I'd put £5 on my phone and text Mum to tell her I was OK, before I went to rescue Tommy. I'd go to his school and snatch him from the playground at morning break.

What would happen after that, I wasn't exactly sure. But it would go something like this: Tommy and me would hitch a lift to the port at Dover and sneak on board a ferry going somewhere hot and sunny faraway. Wherever we landed I'd get a job and support Tommy and me. Then when we'd make our fortunes. When we were adults and couldn't be put into care, we'd come home to Mum and live happily every after. Obviously the plan needed fine-tuning, but it sounded good to me.

The early morning air was cold but – walking fast and with the promise of a McDonald's breakfast and sunnier climes to come – it didn't seem so bad. The February sky was beginning to lighten and, at 7.30, I passed a newsagent that was open for the paperboys to deliver newspapers. I went in and bought £5-worth of phone credit. It wasn't a shop I'd been in much before and the owner didn't know me, so if he wondered why I was out so early he didn't say.

Quarter of an hour later I stepped into the bright lights and warmth of McDonald's. There weren't many customers at this time, just a few workers stopping off for breakfast. I ordered the Big Breakfast, which came with a hot drink – I chose hot chocolate – and I took it to a corner seat well away from the window, which looked out over the High Street. As I ate, I loaded the credit on to my phone and texted Mum. She hadn't replied to the text I'd sent last night and I was getting worried. *R u ok? Txt me. Luv Ryan xxx*. She texted back almost immediately: *Yes, where r u?* I texted back: *Can't say but safe xxx*. She didn't reply and I hoped I hadn't worried her and made her reach for the bottle.

I returned my phone to my jacket pocket and finished my breakfast. I could have eaten it all again easily but that wasn't an option. Having spent £5 on phone credit and £1.99 on the breakfast, I had £3.01 left, and I needed that for later. I hadn't brushed my teeth or washed since yesterday morning and I was beginning to feel dirty. One thing Mum always insisted on, no matter how rubbish our clothes were, was that Tommy and me always brushed our teeth and washed at least once a day, but there was no chance of that right now.

The restaurant was very warm and, now I'd eaten, I was starting to feel more relaxed and a bit sleepy. There was an hour to go before the second part of my plan – rescuing Tommy – could begin. I folded my arms on the table and put my head down. I closed my eyes and must have dropped off without realising it, for suddenly I was woken by a hand on my shoulder shaking me. I looked up to see a McDonald's worker clearing the table.

'Time for school,' he said, trying to be clever.

I checked the clock on the wall: it was exactly nine o'clock. I stood up and, before I left, I went downstairs to the toilets for a pee and a wash. I splashed warm water over my face and rubbed my finger over my teeth, then dried my hands on the hot-air dryer.

Outside, the High Street had come alive since I'd entered McDonald's. Shops were opening and cars and buses crawled up the road in a steady procession. I didn't want to waste money on bus fare, and I still had plenty of time before the next part of my plan, so I decided to walk to Tommy's school. I guessed it was about a mile and half. It's the primary school I went to, so I knew it well. I knew the layout of the building and the routine of the day. I knew which class Tommy was in, and I knew there was a place you could stand – just outside a window – where you could see the kids. They could see you but the teacher couldn't, as long as you were careful. Wayne and me had gone there at the start of term and made faces at the kids through the window until the teacher turned quickly and saw us.

As I walked, I pictured me standing there and Tommy looking up and seeing me. I saw the look of surprise on his face, which would then turn to relief. I could imagine his little face lighting up with happiness as it dawned on him that his big brother had come to rescue him and I gestured to him to meet me by the playground at morning break. I'd chatted to him there when I'd bunked off school before.

Yes, I had it all planned out, and could picture it. Morning break was at 10.20, in an hour's time.

What I hadn't planned for, or pictured, was Tommy's reaction when I explained our escape!

'I'm not going,' he said. 'I don't want to.'

Chapter Nine

'What are you talking about, Tommy?' I said. 'Of course you want to come.'

'No, I don't,' my little brother said, his face up against the wire netting. 'I like it at Mary's. She doesn't get drunk.'

'We're not going back to Mum's,' I hissed. 'We're going on a boat to another country. I'm going to look after you.'

I saw I had his attention now and that of the other kids who were with him. 'Where?' Tommy asked. 'Where you gonna take me? You haven't got money.'

'I have,' I said. 'Look.' Delving into my pocket I pulled out the three £1 coins I'd had as change from my McDonald's.

'That ain't much,' some smart-arse kid standing next to him said. 'I get more than that as pocket money every week.'

'I'm not talking to you,' I snapped. 'Go and play.' I was keeping one eye on the dinner ladies. I knew it wouldn't be long before one of them spotted me and came over to find out what I was doing.

'Tommy, listen to me,' I said anxiously. 'This is what we're going to do. In a minute I want you to go and tell one of the dinner ladies that I have something to give you. Then when she comes and unlocks the gate you grab my hand and we'll make a run for it. You will have to run very fast. Do you understand?' I knew the dinner lady wouldn't be able to leave the other children and come after us. She'd have to go back inside and raise the alarm, by which time we'd be on our way.

Tommy was staring at me, his large brown eyes even wider than ever, like flying saucers. He's such a cute-looking kid.

'Then what?' Smart-arse said. 'What you going to do then?'

'Yeah, what you gonna do then?' Tommy repeated.

'We'll hide until the police stop looking for us,' I said. 'Then we'll get a lift in a lorry to the boat. Once we're on the boat we'll be safe.'

Smart-arse had gone quiet now, clearly impressed by the mention of police, lorry and boat. More impressed than Tommy was.

'Na,' Tommy said, having thought about it. 'I'll stay at Mary's. She gives me loads to eat and I can play with her son, Andrew. He's five, same as me, and he's nice to me.'

'I'm nice to you,' I said, feeling hurt. I decided to change my approach and appeal to Tommy's feelings. I hadn't got long to put my plan into action: once the whistle blew for the end of break Tommy would be back inside the building until the lunch playtime.

'Tommy,' I said, lowering myself to his height and putting my mouth closer to the wire netting. 'I love you, and Mum loves you, but she can't look after us right now. She's upset that we're not together. I'm going to look after you until she's better. I miss you, Tommy. Don't you miss me?'

'Yeah,' Tommy said casually, unfazed, 'but Mary said we'll be seeing each other at contact. You, Mum and me. She told me last night that I hadn't to be upset because we'll all be seeing each other two or three times a week. Didn't your foster carer tell you that?'

In truth, I hadn't stayed long enough at Libby's to find out – not that it would have made any difference to my leaving. I was getting desperate now. One of the dinner ladies had spotted us and kept looking over. I was also annoyed by Tommy's rejection. 'Contact isn't living together,' I said. 'It's just a couple of hours at a centre, and a social worker will be there watching us the whole time.'

'That's what Mary said. She said the social worker was there to make sure we were OK, so Mum can't get drunk again. Mary said I'll be living with her while everything is sorted out. We had sausages, beans and mashed potatoes for dinner last night. Then apple pie and ice cream. What did you have?'

I shrugged. I hadn't had dinner at Libby's. I couldn't blame Tommy for the way he felt. At his age he'd been won over by the promise of regular meals, a kid his own age to play with and an adult looking after him who wasn't drunk or throwing up. He couldn't see the bigger, long-term picture as I could. Or, perhaps, that's all there is to life – food, friendship and someone responsible to look after you?

'Can I help you?' the dinner lady said, finally coming over. She was in her late fifties with very wide hips; she'd been at the school when I was here. 'Oh, it's Ryan,' she said, recognising me. 'You've grown. How are you? Shouldn't you be at school?'

'Na, staff training day,' I lied, hoping she wouldn't notice I was wearing my school uniform.

I looked at Tommy in the faint hope he would change his mind and tell the dinner lady I had something to give him, then we'd make a dash for it. But he didn't.

'Kiss,' he said. 'I'm going to play.' He pursed his lips through the wire netting, ready for me to kiss him. The dinner lady smiled.

I kissed him just as I did every night and every time we said goodbye. Only now of course I wouldn't be kissing him goodnight for a very long time and this goodbye could well be our last.

'See you at contact,' he said, and ran off to play with his mates. The dinner lady smiled again and followed them.

Digging my hands into my trouser pockets, I began to move away from the wire netting. Now what? What the hell was I supposed to do now? I didn't feel like running away without Tommy, but how could I stay? I had nowhere to go and very soon I'd be out of money again. It crossed my mind to go to my school, only a ten-minute walk away. It would be warm and I would get a free dinner, but, after Mum's, I guessed school was the next place the police would look for a runaway.

The school whistle blew behind me for the end of break and I turned and looked at the playground, full of happy smiling kids running to line up. I saw Tommy jostle his way into line, ready to go into the school, and just before he went in he turned and I gave a little wave. He waved back, then disappeared up the steps and into the building. I'd no idea when, or if, I would ever see Tommy again.

With my plans now in shreds and my hope gone, the cold sliced through me like a knife. I guessed it was zero degrees. I sank lower into my jacket and headed back into the town. At least there I could keep warm in the shops until I'd decided what to do.

As I walked, head down against the wind, I suddenly felt very small and alone. In some ways I envied Tommy and his ability to simply accept what was on offer and make the best of it, but at my age I couldn't do that; I thought and worried too much. My family, such as it was, had been torn apart and I was largely to blame. If I'd looked after Tommy better, cleaned the house more, stopped Mum from drinking and kept out of trouble, very likely Duffy would have gone away satisfied and Tommy, me and Mum would still be together. Having a dad would have helped too, I thought. How different our lives would have been with a proper father! Suddenly I felt very angry that my dad hadn't been there for me. The police had computers with information on everyone and there was the internet. He could have traced me if he'd wanted to. So I had to think my father didn't want to know me which is the worst rejection for a boy.

The clock on the old Town Hall showed 11.20 a.m. as I entered the High Street. I went through the revolving doors of Debenham's department store and felt the rush of hot air from the overhead heating duct. I could have happily stood there for the rest of the day, but the security guard to the right was already looking at me. I knew from my previous visits to the shop, when I'd bunked off school before, that – as long as I didn't bring attention to myself or stay too long in one department – I would be left to wander in the warm.

Ten minutes later, I was wandering through the sports department – my favourite, with all the latest gear – when my phone bleeped. My heart sank. It wasn't the bleep of an in-coming text, but that of a low battery. I took the mobile from my pocket and my fears were confirmed: the battery warning light was flashing red. I guessed I had about five minutes before the phone went off completely. The charger was at Mum's. I could have kicked myself for forgetting it.

Then I had a flash of inspiration. Wayne had the same phone as me. Time to ask him for another favour. Before the battery died completely, I texted quickly: *Can I cum after skool 2 charge fone?* I guessed he'd be in lessons now with his phone set to vibrate. I hoped he had his phone in his pocket and not his bag or he wouldn't feel it.

With my mobile in my hand, I continued through to the luggage department, full of expensive suitcases, briefcases, hold-alls and handbags of every size and colour. My phone bleeped again with another low-battery warning, then a few seconds later with an in-coming text.

Wayne: *Sure man, but make it l8er. Old man on nights. Where ru?*

I texted back: *Town. Wot time?*

As I waited for a reply I continued out of the luggage department and into Ladies' Fashion. The minutes passed, as did the rows and rows of expensive dresses, but no text came from Wayne, telling me what time I should go to his house. Then, a few minutes later, my phone gave one final bleep as the battery died and the screen went blank.

Chapter Ten

I left it as late as possible to eat and spend my last £3.01. It was after 3.30 p.m. when, knackered and starving, I finally returned to McDonald's – over seven hours since I'd last eaten and had breakfast. I spent ages carefully choosing from the menu on the wall by the tills. I wanted the most filling food I could get for £3. The girl on the till closest to me waited impatiently.

'Double cheeseburger, fries and a strawberry milkshake,' I said eventually, giving her the three £1 coins.

She handed me 1p change and began dumping the wrapped food on the plastic tray without the least trace of job satisfaction. 'Enjoy your meal,' she said like a robot, as I picked up the tray and moved away.

'Thanks. I will.'

Again, keeping away from the window seats, I sneaked into a corner and wolfed down the food and drink. Then, as luck would have it, a geezer in a suit sitting at the table next to me rushed off after answering his phone, leaving behind his Big Mac with only one bite missing! Leaning over, I grabbed it quickly and wolfed that down as well, followed by his half-drunk tea. I felt like a tramp scouring the bins for leftovers, but at least the extra food would keep me going for a bit.

I didn't know for sure what time I should go to Wayne's but I knew that, when his old man was on nights, he usually left at 6.00 p.m. That was the time me and my mates gathered if we were hanging out there. I'd give his old man fifteen minutes to get clear of the house and aim to be there at 6.15. In the meantime I'd stay in McDonald's for as long as I could.

At 4.00 p.m. kids from school started drifting in, but I didn't know any of them well so they left me alone. I wondered what Tommy was doing. I guessed he'd be in his foster carer's car by now, going 'home'. I wondered if Andrew, her son, was at the same school as Tommy but decided he wasn't: Tommy would have said. I also wondered what Mum was doing but pulled back from that thought. There was nothing I could do to help and worrying about her would only make me more upset.

At just gone 5.00, a waitress pointedly asked if I'd finished and began clearing away the empty food and drink cartons. I shuffled to the end of the seat and went downstairs to use their bog. I had forty five minutes to kill before I could head towards Wayne's. As well as charging my phone I'd ask him if I could stay another night; I'd nowhere else to go. I knew I couldn't keep staying at Wayne's but I was sure he wouldn't mind one more night while I decided what to do. I'd also ask Wayne if I could use his shower. Despite the cold, I'd been sweating with all the walking and I was sure that I was starting to smell.

It was 5.15 when I came up from the bog and left McDonald's. I walked a little way up the High Street and went into the library. I went to the reading room and took a car magazine from the rack, then settled into one of the comfortable armchairs. I'd used the library before when I'd bunked off school. I knew that, as long as I kept my head down and didn't make a noise, I could stay there for a very long time. The warmth and comfort of the place, together with the thought of a shower, charging my phone and another night with my best mate, lifted my spirits. Lifted them out of the despair I was starting to feel – until I got to Wayne's, that is.

* * *

I must have had a sixth sense or perhaps, without noticing it, I'd heard a noise. Because, instead of marching straight up to Wayne's back door where I was expecting to find him waiting, I slowed my pace and kept low. I crept up to the kitchen window and peered in. The kitchen light was on and, set against the dark outside, the room was on display.

Straight in front of me was the old table, covered, as usual, with used mugs, empty beer cans, and dirty plates. As I turned my head and peered further in, to my left, at the far end of the kitchen, I saw Wayne. At the same time, he cried out. I froze. Fear shot through me.

His old man had Wayne pinned up against the wall with one hand and was beating the shit out of him with the other. Wayne's cheeks were stained with tears and his right eye was already starting to swell. He tried to move his head to get out of the way of the next blow but failed, and cried out again.

'You'll do as I say, next time. Won't you, laddy?' the pig shouted in Wayne's face. I saw Wayne was trying to nod but his head was held fast by his dad. His fist landed on the side of Wayne's head again. I winced and pulled back. I couldn't just stand there and watch, but there was little I could do beyond distracting the old man in the hope he would let go of Wayne. Clenching my fist, I banged hard on the window, then ran like hell. I was already in the alley when I heard the back door crash open and Wayne's dad yell: 'Wait till I get 'old of you, ya little bleeder. You won't know what's hit ya.'

I continued running and hoped I'd given Wayne the chance to get away, though fuck knows where he would go now that he couldn't hide at my place. I ran down the alleyways until I'd put a safe distance between his house and me; then I slowed to a walk. I was hot and trembling – from fear, and anger at seeing my best mate being beaten up by his pig of a father.

So that was how Wayne had got his cuts and bruises, I realised. He'd often arrived in school looking like he'd been in a car crash but, when one of us kids or a teacher had asked him what had happened, he said he'd been fighting with kids on the estate. We'd believed him. Like me, he has a reputation for getting into trouble sometimes but, now I knew the truth, I felt so stupid. How blind and thoughtless I'd been!

I remembered the nights that Wayne had come round to my house to escape his dad's threats but it had never struck me that he'd actually been beating him up. Wayne hadn't been cut or bruised when he'd arrived at my house, but of course he wouldn't have been – those were the times when he'd escaped. It was the other times when he hadn't managed to escape when he'd been done over. Jesus! Why the fuck hadn't he confided in me and said something? I knew the answer of course. Wayne hadn't told me about his dad for the same reason I hadn't told him about the worst of my mum's drinking – pride.

Still shaking from what I'd seen, I continued walking up and down the estate's back alleys. I was tempted to return to Wayne's house and make sure he was OK, but decided against it. If his old man saw me there, it would be worse for Wayne (and me) and there was nothing I could to do to help him. I was in as much shit as he was – probably more. I just hoped he'd got away.

With my phone dead, I had no way of telling the time, but I guessed it was about 7.00 p.m. It was dark and the winter air was getting very cold, ready for another freezing night. I'd no money – apart from 2 p – and nowhere to go.

My little brother, Tommy, was safe and warm at his foster carer's, probably on his way to bed.

My mate, Wayne, was God knows where. And, as for Mum? I thought of Mum and tears formed in my eyes.

Chapter Eleven

I completed another large circle of the estate; there weren't many people using the alleyways, now it was getting late. Then I began towards the terrace, Conker Lane, which – until yesterday – had been my home. How long ago 'home' now seemed with everything that had happened!

Only yesterday morning I'd woken Tommy and helped him dress and wash before a neighbour took him and her own kids to school. Then I'd checked on Mum, who, after she had set fire to her bed with her cigarette end, had spent the rest of the night on the sofa sleeping off the drink. And, finally, I'd got myself to school, never dreaming social services were plotting to take Tommy and me away from home for good.

I arrived at the end of the alley closest to Conker Lane and peered out gingerly, looking for police cars. The coast was clear. I made my way to the end of the terrace and went round the back. The layout of our terrace is different from Wayne's: he has his kitchen at the back but that's where our living room is. Most of the houses in the terrace had their downstairs' lights on and the curtains open, showing little scenes of family life: kids sitting on sofas in front of a television or PlayStation, a father reading a newspaper, a mother sipping from a mug. Not so in my house, I thought bitterly; and it never was.

I arrived at our back door. Surprisingly, the light wasn't on and I wondered if Mum was out, but I couldn't imagine where she'd have gone. I tried the door handle and it opened. Little wonder Mum gets taken advantage of – she's far too trusting.

I knew I wasn't doing myself (or Mum) any favours by coming home, but I was almost past caring. With no family, my plans for running away with Tommy in ruins and knowing my best mate had been beaten up regularly by his father, life didn't really seem worth living. Also, seeing Wayne like that, had made me realise that Mum wasn't so bad. Yes, she drank heavily and I guess she neglected us, but she'd never once hit Tommy or me, not even when I'd caused her trouble. Underneath all the drinking, she was a good, kind person who loved us, and I loved her. I knew I had to tell her that before I went away.

Going in, and not knowing what state I'd find Mum in, I closed and locked the back door before I switched on the light. Mum jumped. She was sitting at one end of the sofa in the dark. As soon as she saw me she came over and hugged me hard.

'Ryan, Ryan, love, I've been worried sick. Where have you been?' Her hair was crumpled and she was in the clothes she'd been wearing yesterday, so I guessed she hadn't gone to bed. 'I love you, son,' she said.

'I love you too, Mum,' I said and squeezed her tight.

As we hugged I looked around the room for empty bottles – the tell-tale signs she'd been drinking heavily – but I couldn't see any. I couldn't smell drink on her either and she seemed reasonably steady in my arms, although very frail and upset.

'I've been worried sick,' she said again, drawing back slightly. 'The social worker said you weren't in school, and the police put out a missing person's notice. I tried to phone your mobile but it was off. It's been off all afternoon.'

'The battery's flat,' I said. It was then I noticed the cut on her forehead, partly hidden by her fringe. 'What happened?' I asked, lifting her hair away for a better look.

'It's nothing,' she said, embarrassed, pulling her fringe down again to cover the gash. I knew she must have fallen the previous night while drunk. It had happened before. 'I'll live,' she said.

I looked at her steadily. 'You won't if you don't stop drinking, Mum,' I said, deathly seriously. 'The drink will kill you and kill you very soon.'

She took her hand from my arm and moved slightly away. 'Come and sit down, son,' she said quietly. 'I need to talk to you.'

I went with her to the sofa and we both sat down. I looked at her sad profile as she rested her elbows on her knees. Looking down, she concentrated on the floor as she spoke.

'Ryan, love, you are old enough for me to speak to you like an adult,' she began. 'Goodness knows, you've had the responsibility of one with me being like this. The social worker was here this afternoon.'

I tried to interrupt but Mum raised her hand, motioning for me to listen. 'Duffy was here for two hours earlier and what she said was right, although I didn't want to hear it to begin with. She said my drinking was stopping me looking after you boys properly. It has been doing so for some time, which is why social services have been monitoring us.'

I went to butt in again but Mum shook her head. 'No, hear me out, Ryan. Duffy was right. If it hadn't been for you, you and Tommy would have been taken into care a long while ago. I'm grateful for all you did, but I haven't been a mother to either of you. How could I be? I've been drunk for most of the time. Duffy said I now had the chance to get my life sorted out. They are going to fund a rehab programme to help get me off the drink. She said they'll give me a year to get dry and get this place cleared up. She said they will monitor my progress and if, at the end of the year, I am doing well, social services will assess me with a view to having you both back.'

'And you believe them, Mum?' I finally cut in. 'You'll never get us back! They'll see to that.'

'I will,' Mum said quietly, raising her eyes to mine. 'I believe them, and I've got to believe in myself. I think having you two taken into care has given me the shock I needed to get off the drink once and for all. You can help me by keeping out of trouble and going to school. If you do that, then we will both be working towards you and Tommy coming home.'

I held her gaze. There was a truthfulness in her eyes and a determination in her voice that I couldn't remember seeing those other times when she'd promised to give up the drink before. Could this time be different? Could she do it this time around? I almost believed she might manage it for, unlike all of her previous promises to stop drinking, this vow was made while she was actually sober.

'But I miss you and Tommy,' I said. 'It's not fair that we were split up.'

'I know, love, and it's something I shall be speaking to my solicitor about.'

'You've got a solicitor?' I asked, amazed and impressed. 'When? Where? How?'

She gave a small laugh and took my hand in hers. 'I phoned the Citizens' Advice Bureau and they gave me the name of a firm of solicitors who specialise in family law. I phoned them this afternoon after Duffy had gone. I have an appointment with a solicitor tomorrow.'

I didn't know what to say. I'd never seen this side of Mum before – sober, taking charge and getting organised.

'As well as working out contact arrangements,' she continued, 'my solicitor will be asking the judge to have the two of you placed together while you are in care. He said there is a good chance of this happening. Apparently judges prefer siblings to be kept together, unless there is a good reason why they shouldn't be, and there isn't here.'

'No,' I said. 'I love Tommy. I wouldn't hurt him.'

'Exactly.' Mum patted my hand gently. 'Now, Ryan, I know it's going to be difficult for us all, but I have a year to prove to the social, you, Tommy and myself that I can do this. I need you to be brave and do as I say. In a minute, when we've finished talking, I'm going to make you a hot chocolate. Then I'm going to phone the duty social worker and tell them you're here and ready to return to your foster carer.'

I went to protest again – I wanted to stay with Mum and help her get better – but Mum was shaking her head. 'No, Ryan,' she said firmly. 'I'm doing what is best for you. I'm not having a son of mine hanging round the streets in the day and dossing wherever he can at night. You will be well looked after at Libby's, and don't go giving me that crap about not fitting in because of race. It might have worked with the social but it won't with me.' She gave a knowing smile and waited for my response.

I smiled back and then, very slowly, I nodded. 'You're my Mum, and I'll do whatever you think is best.'

Chapter Twelve

'And there's me thinking it was the smell of my cooking that made you run away,' Libby said, laughing. 'Clearly it wasn't!'

It was nearly 10 o'clock at night and I was sitting at the table in Libby's dining room, eating my second helping of her cottage pie. There was just Libby and me at the table. Her son, Brendon, was in bed asleep and her other foster child, Callum, was in his room watching television. Libby had eaten earlier with Brendon and Callum and was now sitting with me while I ate, explaining about being in care and what would happen – short and long term.

'Your social worker will phone tomorrow,' Libby continued, 'to give us the contact arrangements – when you will see your mum and brother. It will seem strange to start with, meeting at the centre, but it will begin to feel fine after a week or so. I've been through this so many times before with the children I've looked after; trust me, everything will be all right.' Libby was adding this 'trust me, I've done it before, everything will be all right' to most of what she was telling me about being in care, and I was beginning to believe her. She had a reassuring way with her that made you trust her and believe what she said. I was starting to feel a bit better.

The duty social worker had brought me to Libby's about half an hour before and I'd gone straight up to 'my' bedroom and put my mobile on charge. I'd texted Wayne as soon as my phone was plugged in but he hadn't replied, and I was really worried about him. Supposing he hadn't got away from his evil dad? Mum's suitcase was on top of the wardrobe in the room and, when I opened the wardrobe doors, I found that all my clothes from the case had been washed and ironed and were hanging neatly on hangers.

'How did you know I would be coming back?' I now asked Libby as I ate my tea.

She smiled. 'Instinct, but if you hadn't, at least your clothes would have been clean when I packed them.'

I wondered if I could now ask Libby about the pocket money, which was no longer under my pillow. I was trying hard to be polite for Mum's sake, and I didn't want to upset Libby on my first night. Would it be rude to ask her for my pocket money now, I wondered?

I listened nicely until Libby had finished telling me that we would be going shopping after school tomorrow to buy me a coat, school shoes, new trainers and anything else I needed, before I said: 'I don't have any money at all.'

She gave another little laugh; Libby laughed easily. 'No, well,' she said matter-of-factly, 'that's what happens when you run off in the middle of the night. You will have your pocket money on Saturday, the same as Callum and Brendon. *After* you've completed a good week at school. There's only one day left, so it shouldn't be too difficult.' She smiled kindly, but I knew she meant exactly what she said. 'And, Ryan, like I said before, if you need anything in the meantime, ask me and I'll get it for you. Does that sound fair?'

I nodded. 'I'd like to phone my best mate, Wayne, please,' I said. 'He was in trouble earlier and I want to make sure he's all right. I've only got a couple of texts left. Can I use the house phone to ring his mobile and leave a message?'

'Of course,' Libby said. 'And once you've settled in, Wayne can come and visit you here; stay for some dinner; and sleepover sometimes if he likes.'

I was warming to Libby and, whilst I'd obviously rather have been at home with Mum,

I knew I had to make the best of it here for all our sakes. Libby took away my empty plate and returned from the kitchen with a bowl of treacle pudding and custard. That made me warm to her even more.

'Leave what you don't want,' she said, laughing, as I quickly set upon it, ladling in spoonful after spoonful, and the bowl emptied quickly.

The phone rang – from an extension on the sideboard.

'I wonder who that can be at this time?' Libby said, going to answer it. 'Hello?' she said, tentatively, then smiled: 'Oh, hi, Joyce. How are you?' So I guessed it was a friend of hers.

It went quiet as Libby listened to what the caller was saying and I carefully scraped the last of the custard from the bowl and wondered if it would be rude to lick the bowl clean.

'You don't say!' Libby exclaimed into the phone, her voice rising with astonishment. 'Well, well! Now there's something! Yes, I'm sure he would, Joyce. Just a minute. Ryan,' Libby said, taking the phone from her ear and turning to me. She was smiling and looked very pleased with herself. 'Did you say your best mate was called Wayne? Is it Wayne Andrews?'

My mouth fell open in astonishment. 'Yes. How did you know his second name?'

She grinned. 'You won't have to phone him. He's phoning you. Come on, he's with Joyce.'

'Wayne?' I said, unable to understand exactly what Libby was telling me.

'Yes, come on.'

I stood and nearly tripped over the chair in my eagerness to get to the phone.

'He's here,' Libby said into the phone, then passed it to me.

'Wayne?' I said.

'Hey, man!'

'Wayne, where are you?'

'With a foster carer, called Joyce. I'm in care, man, same as you!' Whereas I'd been angry and upset when I'd first been taken into care, Wayne sounded happy and very relieved. 'All the foster carers know each other, man,' he said. 'So when I told Joyce about my mate Ryan, she guessed it was you who was staying at Libby's.'

I glanced at Libby, who was clearing the table, and gave her the thumbs-up sign.

'But what happened?' I asked Wayne. 'How did you end up at Joyce's? I saw you through your kitchen window.'

'Yeah, man, I knew it was you banging on the window. I'd gone down to the kitchen about five minutes before, to warn you not to come in as the old man had thrown a sickie and wasn't going in to work. But he was already down there, hitting the bottle. He grabbed me by the throat and laid into me. It's not the first time, man. When you banged on the glass, he let go of me and I ran out the front door and up the road to a neighbour. She's looked after me before, but when she saw my face she said it had gone too far. She called the social and the police, and they brought me here. I haven't got any of my things, but Joyce says we will sort that out tomorrow. So how are you, man?'

'OK,' I said, and it was true.

Wayne and I rabbited on for about twenty minutes. Wayne did most of the talking – about how good it was to be at Joyce's. Then Libby said it was my bedtime and I had to finish on the phone. I was going to argue: I never went to bed at Mum's before midnight and it was only 10.30, but I heard Joyce telling Wayne the same at the other end of the phone and he wound up.

'Got to go, man,' he said. 'Joyce is making me a hot drink before bed. See you tomorrow at school?'

'You bet!'

I hung up, feeling maybe life wasn't so bad after all. All I needed now was to persuade Libby to buy me a bigger bed so Tommy could come and live with us, and we'd be fine, until Mum got herself sorted out and could look after us again.

'Bathroom for you, young man,' Libby said, heading out of the dining room. I followed. 'I've put clean pyjamas on your bed, and a toothbrush, toothpaste and soap with your towel in the bathroom. Even though it's late, you're having a shower tonight. You don't look sparkling clean to me.' She laughed.

'I don't feel it either,' I admitted.

I was about to go upstairs when suddenly I heard a noise from behind. I span round and stared at the front door, my senses on red alert.

'Don't worry,' Libby said. 'That'll be my hubby, Fynn, returning from the late shift. You haven't met him yet, so say hi before you go up; then the two of you can get to know each other better at the weekend.'

I waited as the key turned in the front door and Libby went down the hall to greet her old man. The door opened and he stepped inside. She kissed him on the cheek. 'Fynn, love, this is Ryan,' she said. 'He's the lad I told you about who's staying with us until his mum gets better.'

Fynn nodded at me and came down the hall with his hand outstretched, ready to shake mine. My mouth fell open and I stared at him in disbelief. I couldn't believe my eyes! Fynn was tall and black like Libby, but that wasn't the reason I was staring. It was what he was wearing that had shocked me.

'Good to meet you, Ryan,' he said, shaking my hand warmly.

'And you,' I managed to mumble.

'I've one more late shift tomorrow,' he said, 'then I've got the weekend off. I've promised to take Callum and Brendon to the match on Saturday. You up for that?'

I nodded, still gawping at what he wore – his uniform. 'I don't believe it!' I said at last.

'What's that?' Fynn asked, puzzled, glancing at Libby.

'That my foster dad's a policeman!'

'Well, you better believe it,' Fynn said, laughing. 'So keep out of trouble.'

'I will.'

'Good lad.'

Postscript

I asked Libby if she would buy a bigger bed so Tommy could come and live with us, but she said no because she was thinking of buying bunk beds, which would be more comfortable; then she explained. She said my Mum had seen a solicitor, and the following week they were going to court when there was a good chance that the judge would make a ruling that Tommy and me should be placed in care together.

Libby was right. The judge said that Tommy and me should stay in foster care whilst Mum went into rehab, but it was important that siblings stayed together whenever possible. So because Libby had offered to have us both, Tommy could move in with me.

A year on we're still living with Libby and Fynn, and will do until Mum is better. We get to see Mum twice a week – on Wednesdays after school and on Sundays. For the first three months, we had to see Mum at the Contact Centre with a social worker present which I didn't like but then it was changed to what Duffy calls 'community contact'.

So now we see Mum away from the centre and without another adult watching over us. We do fun things with Mum that we didn't do before, like going to the cinema, ice-skating and bowling. Sometimes Mum collects us from Libby and Fynn's and sometimes Libby or Fynn drops us off wherever we're meeting Mum. Libby and Mum have become good friends and I know they sometimes chat on the phone in the evening when I'm in bed. Mum is getting better slowly and, although Duffy says she is making good progress, she isn't there yet so the social are giving her more time to get well so she can have me and Tommy back.

Tommy and me get on well with our foster dad, Fynn. He does all the things a dad should do and we've both decided we're going to join the police when we're older. Fynn is teaching me how to control my anger so when I feel hot and twitchy, rather than hit someone, I take a few deep breaths, count to ten and walk away. Me and Tommy go to school every day. Some days I'd rather not, but if I don't go to school, I don't get my pocket money (which went up to £10 when I had my thirteenth birthday) so I go along and try to do the work and behave myself.

One Saturday morning when I'd been at Libby's for about two months, I caught a 247 bus to go and meet up with Wayne. I thought the geezer driving the bus looked vaguely familiar but it didn't click who he was until he said, not unkindly; 'So are you going to pay your fare this time?' I realised it was the same bus driver who'd let me off the fare on that dreadful night when I'd run away from Libby's and had no money.

'Of course I am,' I said proudly. 'I've got a bus pass now. And money, so I can pay you what I owe you.'

'Good lad,' he said.

I showed him the bus pass Libby had arranged for me; then, returning it safely to my pocket, I took out a £1 coin.

'Here's my fare for last time,' I said. 'Thanks for helping me out back then.' I held out the coin.

'You're welcome,' the driver said. 'You look a lot better than you did that night. I guess things are working out for you?'

'They are.'

'I tell you what. How about you put that £1 in a charity box? You did the right thing by offering me the money you owed, but it will only mess up my till.'

'Sure. Will do,' I said. 'And thanks again.'

And I did just what I told the driver I would do.

The following Saturday I was in town, shopping with Libby, and there was a woman in the High Street collecting money for starving children in Africa. The tin she held had a picture on it of a scrawny kid with a big swollen belly and it reminded me of my promise to the friendly bus driver. The photo also made me think how lucky I was – I could have been that kid if I'd be born in Africa. I took £1 from my pocket and then I took another £1 out and dropped them both in the tin. The woman thanked me and I could see Libby was impressed by my generosity – but not half as impressed as I was with myself!

If you would like to know what happened to Ryan after this story was published, you can read an update on my website, www.cathyglass. co.uk. Click on 'Books' and *My Dad's A Policeman*.

Quick Reads 📖

Books in the Quick Reads series

101 Ways to get your Child to Read	Patience Thomson
All These Lonely People	Gervase Phinn
Black-Eyed Devils	Catrin Collier
Bloody Valentine	James Patterson
Buster Fleabags	Rolf Harris
The Cave	Kate Mosse
Chickenfeed	Minette Walters
Cleanskin	Val McDermid
Clouded Vision	Linwood Barclay
A Cool Head	Ian Rankin
Danny Wallace and the Centre of the Universe	Danny Wallace
The Dare	John Boyne
Doctor Who: Code of the Krillitanes	Justin Richards
Doctor Who: I Am a Dalek	Gareth Roberts
Doctor Who: Made of Steel	Terrance Dicks
Doctor Who: Revenge of the Judoon	Terrance Dicks
Doctor Who: The Sontaran Games	Jacqueline Rayner
Dragons' Den: Your Road to Success	
A Dream Come True	Maureen Lee
Follow Me	Sheila O'Flanagan
Girl on the Platform	Josephine Cox
The Grey Man	Andy McNab
The Hardest Test	Scott Quinnell
Hell Island	Matthew Reilly

Hello Mum	Bernardine Evaristo
How to Change Your Life in 7 Steps	John Bird
Humble Pie	Gordon Ramsay
Jack and Jill	Lucy Cavendish
Kung Fu Trip	Benjamin Zephaniah
Last Night Another Soldier	Andy McNab
Life's New Hurdles	Colin Jackson
Life's Too Short	Val McDermid, Editor
Lily	Adèle Geras
Men at Work	Mike Gayle
Money Magic	Alvin Hall
My Dad's a Policeman	Cathy Glass
One Good Turn	Chris Ryan
The Perfect Holiday	Cathy Kelly
The Perfect Murder	Peter James
RaW Voices: True Stories of Hardship	Vanessa Feltz
Reaching for the Stars	Lola Jaye
Reading My Arse!	Ricky Tomlinson
Star Sullivan	Maeve Binchy
Strangers on the 16:02	Priya Basil
The Sun Book of Short Stories	
Survive the Worst and Aim for the Best	Kerry Katona
The 10 Keys to Success	John Bird
Tackling Life	Charlie Oatway
The Tannery	Sherrie Hewson
Traitors of the Tower	Alison Weir
Trouble on the Heath	Terry Jones
Twenty Tales of the War Zone	John Simpson
We Won the Lottery	Danny Buckland

Quick Reads 📖

Great stories, great writers, great entertainment

Quick Reads are brilliantly written short new books by bestselling authors and celebrities. Whether you're an avid reader who wants a quick fix or haven't picked up a book since school, sit back, relax and let Quick Reads inspire you.

We would like to thank all our partners in the Quick Reads project for their help and support:

Arts Council England
The Department for Business, Innovation and Skills
NIACE
unionlearn
National Book Tokens
The Reading Agency
National Literacy Trust
Welsh Books Council
Basic Skills Cymru, Welsh Assembly Government
The Big Plus Scotland
DELNI
NALA

Quick Reads would also like to thank the Department for Business, Innovation and Skills; Arts Council England and World Book Day for their sponsorship and NIACE for their outreach work.

Quick Reads is a World Book Day initiative.
www.quickreads.org.uk   www.worldbookday.com

Quick Reads 📖

Great stories, great writers, great entertainment

Follow Me

Sheila O'Flanagan

Headline Review

The romantic tale of a career girl, a handsome
stranger and chips

Pippa Jones is 20-something and single. She likes chips,
country music and her cat. She also loves her career as
number one sales rep for a computer firm. The only
thing she hasn't got time for is men. Broken-hearted last
time round, Pippa is sticking to girlfriends – and winning
a dream trip to New York.

However, life isn't that simple. A rival firm is stealing her
clients, and a tall, fair stranger is following her
everywhere. He's in the bar, at dinner, even at her
meetings. Is he a stalker? Whoever he is, he's about to
turn Pippa's world upside down

Other resources

Enjoy this book? Find out about all the others from
www.quickreads.org.uk

Free courses are available for anyone who wants to
develop their skills. You can attend the courses in your
local area. If you'd like to find out more, phone
0800 66 0800.

Don't get by get on 0800 66 0800

For more information on developing your basic skills in
Scotland, call The Big Plus free on 0808 100 1080 or visit
www.thebigplus.com

Join the Reading Agency's Six Book Challenge at
www.sixbookchallenge.org.uk

read
readingagency.org.uk

Publishers Barrington Stoke (www.barringtonstoke.co.uk)
and New Island (www.newisland.ie) also provide books
for new readers.

Barrington Stoke

OPEN DOOR

The BBC runs an adult basic skills campaign.
See www.bbc.co.uk/raw.

BBC
raw
skills for everyday life

www.worldbookday.com